S0-AJJ-158

THE BIGGEST PARADE

ELIZABETH WINTHROP

ILLUSTRATED BY
MARK ULRIKSEN

Henry Holt and Company • New York

One day in June, the mayor of Bonesport knocked on Fred and Harvey's door.

"The town is two hundred and fifty years old," she said to Harvey. "We want to have the biggest parade Bonesport has ever seen, so we made you parade chairman."

Harvey was so excited. He loved parades! Fred did not.

The last time Fred was in a parade, someone
put a baby on his back, and someone tied a flag
to his tail, and . . .

. . . someone blew a horn in his ear.

Fred couldn't hear for a week.

As soon as the mayor left, Harvey started a list. "Mrs. Hemlock will be the grand marshal," he said to Fred. "She and Mrs. Meacham will lead the parade in their convertible with their cat, Matahari. The Little League team will ride on a float. Their mascot, Hawkeye, can be dressed as an umpire. I'll make his costume myself."

Fred groaned. His friend Hawkeye wouldn't be caught dead in an umpire costume.

The list got longer and longer. By dinnertime, every dog and person and horse in Bonesport was in the parade. Except one . . . Fred!

Frank
Paula
Barbara
Syd
John
Brian
Mark
Dick
Hans

"You will lead the parade dressed as the founding dog of Bonesport."

Fred shook his head.

"Then you can ride with Mrs. Meacham and Mrs. Hemlock and Matahari."

Fred shook his head again. Matahari was a wild and crazy cat.

"Then you and the mayor can bring up the rear."

Good heavens, no, thought Fred. He sat down to munch on a liver treat.

But Fred loved Harvey.
He helped him paint posters,
hang out flags, and sew costumes.

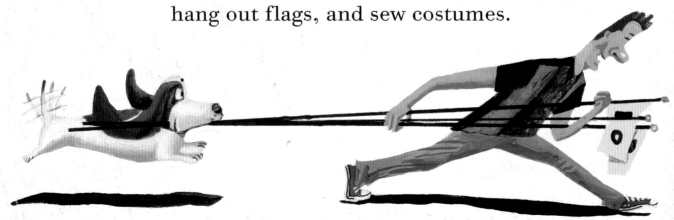

He even made Hawkeye stand still for his fittings.

The morning of the parade, Harvey got up very early. He shined his buttons and checked his list. He blew his whistle over and over again until Fred's ears stood straight up in the air.

"Come on, Fred," Harvey begged. "You can ride with Hawkeye on the baseball float."

Fred shook his head one last time. He gave Harvey a big lick on his ear and stood in the doorway waving good-bye with his tail.

Never had Bonesport seen such a parade.
Flags flapped in the wind. Children rang their
bicycle bells. Horses snapped their braided tails.
Mrs. Meacham honked her horn. Matahari sat
on Mrs. Hemlock's hat.

The marching band tuned their instruments.
Everything was perfect. Except for one thing . . .
one *very* important thing.

Every person and horse and dog
in Bonesport was IN the parade, so
there was nobody left in Bonesport
to WATCH the parade.

Nobody to cheer and howl and
stamp. Nobody to bark and whistle.
Except for one . . .

FRED!

Harvey blew his whistle.
Mrs. Meacham revved her engine.
Matahari yowled.
Hawkeye barked.
The marching band struck up a tune.

As soon as the parade began, Fred jumped up and
down in his seat and howled and flapped his ears.
He stamped and whistled and stood on his back
legs until the very last marcher had disappeared
over the very last hill.

It was the BIGGEST parade the
town of Bonesport had ever seen.

And Fred was the NOISIEST
audience the town had ever heard.

For Mindy Hackner who loves books,
dogs, and parades!
—E. W.

To my very savvy little art directors
and models, Emma and Lily
—M. U.

Henry Holt and Company, LLC, *Publishers since 1866*
175 Fifth Avenue, New York, New York 10010
www.henryholtchildrensbooks.com

Henry Holt® is a registered trademark of
Henry Holt and Company, LLC.
Text copyright © 2006 by Elizabeth Winthrop
Illustrations copyright © 2006 by Mark Ulriksen
All rights reserved.
Distributed in Canada by H. B. Fenn and Company Ltd.

Library of Congress Cataloging-in-Publication Data
Winthrop, Elizabeth.
The biggest parade / Elizabeth Winthrop;
illustrated by Mark Ulriksen.—1st ed.
p.   cm.
Summary: Harvey is so excited when the mayor appoints him
Parade Chairman for a big celebration that he forgets something
very important but, fortunately, his dog, Fred, remembers.
ISBN-13: 978-0-8050-7685-1 / ISBN-10: 0-8050-7685-9
[1. Parades—Fiction. 2. Dogs—Fiction. 3. Pets—Fiction.]
I. Ulriksen, Mark, ill. II. Title.
PZ7.W768Big 2006   [E]—dc22   2005019753

First Edition—2006
The artist used acrylic paints on watercolor paper
to create the illustrations for this book.
Printed in the United States of America on acid-free paper. ∞

1 3 5 7 9 10 8 6 4 2